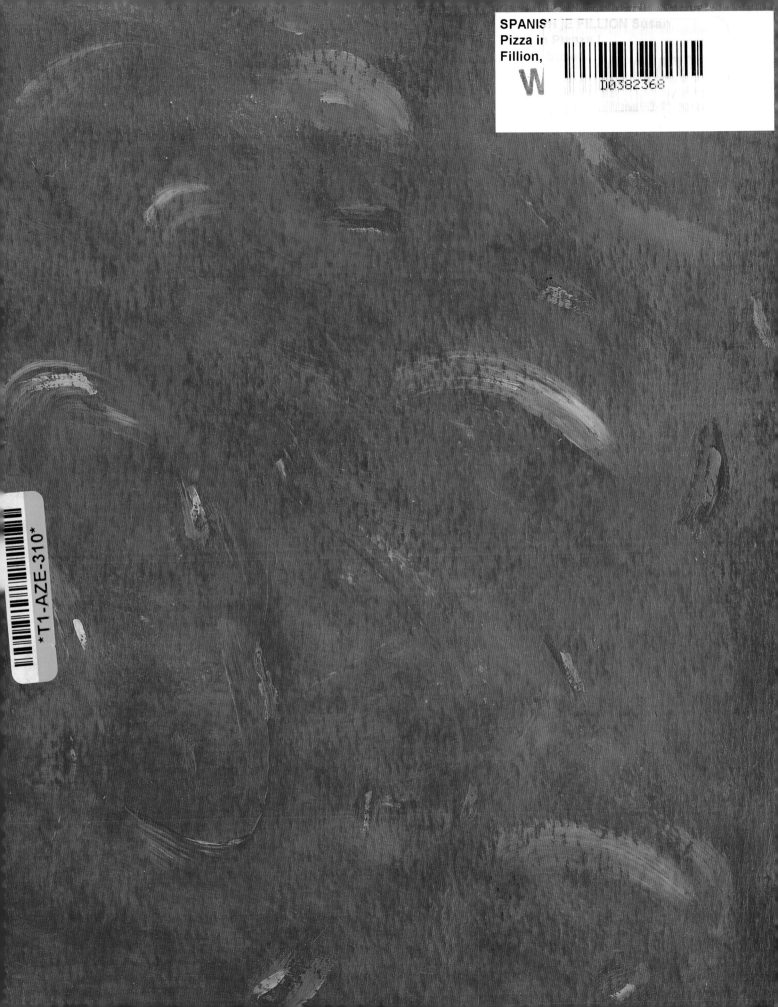

Pizza in Pienza

Pizza in Pienza

by Susan Fillion

DAVID R. GODINE · *Publisher* · *Boston*

This is Queen Margherita of Italy in the year 1889.

⮞⮞⮞

Questa è la regina Margherita d'Italia nell'anno 1889.

And this is me sitting on the steps in front of my house today.

E questa sono io oggi, seduta sugli scalini davanti a casa mia.

I live in Pienza, a small town in Italy where Pope Pius II was born.

Vivo a Pienza, una piccola cittadina in Italia dov'è nato Papa Pio II.

This is the main town square and our little cathedral.

Ecco la piazza principale con la nostra piccola cattedrale.

My family has been here for many generations.

La mia famiglia vive qui da molte generazioni.

Life here is still pretty old-fashioned.

La vita qui è ancora abbastanza tradizionale.

The trucks are small, the policemen ride horses,
and people walk everywhere.

*Gli autocarri sono piccoli, i poliziotti vanno a cavallo
e la gente va a piedi dappertutto.*

On Saturday mornings, I go to the outdoor market
where I know almost everyone.

*Il sabato mattina vado al mercato
dove conosco quasi tutti.*

My favorite place to go is Giovanni's, and my favorite food is pizza.
I close my eyes and breathe in all the warm and savory smells.

Il mio posto preferito è Da Giovanni e il mio cibo preferito è la pizza.
Chiudo gli occhi e respiro il suo caldo profumo e il suo sapore.

I love to eat pizza anywhere, anytime.
Even when it rains, I eat it walking in the street.

Mi piace mangiare la pizza ovunque e in qualunque momento.
La mangio camminando per strada, anche quando piove.

Here in Italy, we eat our main meal at midday.

Qui in Italia, il pasto principale è a mezzogiorno.

Everyone comes home from school and work to eat and talk.

Tutti tornano a casa da scuola e dal lavoro per mangiare e fare due chiacchiere.

Even while I'm eating spaghetti, I'm dreaming about the next pizza pie.

෧෩෨෫෨

Anche mentre mangio gli spaghetti sogno la mia prossima pizza.

I've asked my grandmother to teach me how to make it by hand . . .

Ho chiesto a mia nonna di insegnarmi come farla a mano . . .

. . . just like Giovanni who cooks it in a brick oven heated by a wood fire.

. . . proprio come Giovanni che la cuoce nel forno a legna.

After school, I walk to the library to read about the history of pizza.

Dopo scuola vado in biblioteca a leggere la storia della pizza.

Incredible! I discover that the story of pizza is old. Very old, in fact.

෨෨෨෨

Incredibile! Scopro che la storia della pizza è antica. Davvero molto antica.

Ancient Greeks and Italians ate flatbreads with onions, herbs, and honey.

Gli antichi greci e gli italiani mangiavano la focaccia con cipolle, erbette e miele.

And many Mediterranean cultures, from Egyptians and Babylonians to Armenians and Israelites, have been eating some type of pizza for centuries.

E molti popoli del Mediterraneo, da egizi e babilonesi, ad armeni ed israeliti, hanno mangiato per secoli diversi tipi di pizza.

But pizza as we know it was really born in Naples, Italy.

Ma la pizza come la conosciamo noi è nata in realtà a Napoli, in Italia.

At first it was a peasant food, sold by the slice in the street.

୧ଓୱ୭

All'inizio era un piatto contadino venduto al taglio per strada.

The tomato came to Italy sometime in the 1500s from South America . . .
maybe with Christopher Columbus, who was Italian.

Il pomodoro è arrivato in Italia dal Sud America intorno al 1500 . . .
forse con Cristoforo Colombo, che era italiano.

Mozzarella cheese was made from the milk of water buffalos,
probably imported from Asia.

*La mozzarella veniva fatta con il latte di bufale d'acqua,
probabilmente importate dall'Asia.*

Then a famous pizza maker in Naples invented the Pizza Margherita:
green, white, and red, like the new Italian flag,
and named after the Queen herself.

*Poi un famoso pizzaiolo di Napoli ha inventato la pizza Margherita:
verde, bianca e rossa, proprio come la nuova bandiera Italiana
e chiamata così in onore della regina.*

The first pizzeria in the United States opened in New York City in 1905.

La prima pizzeria negli Stati Uniti ha aperto a New York nel 1905.

But pizza really became popular after the Second World War.
Soldiers returning from Italy talked about it when they got home.
Everyone wanted to try it.

ରେଖେଡେଖ

Ma la pizza è diventata davvero famosa solo dopo la seconda guerra mondiale.
I soldati di ritorno dall'Italia ne parlavano una volta a casa.
Tutti la volevano provare.

Now there is pizza in Pienza . . .

Ora c'è la pizza a Pienza . . .

. . . and all around the world!

. . . *e in tutto il mondo!*

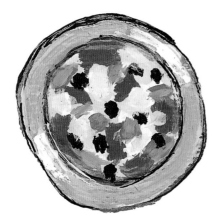

A Note from the Author/Illustrator

Many people have asked me, "Why pizza?" and "Why Pienza?" My answer is that these are two of my favorite things. For years I have been making pizza at home on Friday nights for my family and friends. I used to have lists taped to the kitchen cabinet reminding me which of my kids' friends liked or did not like certain toppings. Often, there would be a small team of pizza-makers spreading dough by hand and arguing about which toppings to use. Those were the days! I love it when my grown children, nieces, and nephews, who now make their own pizzas, call me with questions.

And Pienza is a place I fell in love with years ago. It is a sturdy and captivating small town, off the beaten path in Tuscany. The birthplace of Pope Pius II, Pienza was rebuilt on the Pope's orders as a tribute to himself, and it remains an enchanting Renaissance gem.

One day I had the idea of combining a story about contemporary life in this town with a brief history of pizza. PIZZA in PIENZA ... the words just seemed to go together. As I wrote the story, I found myself translating it into Italian in my mind, and I was amused by the many similarities between the languages. You can almost understand the Italian simply by reading the English. So, I decided to make the book bilingual. *Ecco!*

A Note on Pronunciation

Italian is fairly easy to pronounce. It is a wonderful, musical language in which most words are pronounced the way they look. Nearly every letter is clearly enunciated: for example, *forse* is pronounced *for'-say*, and *tradizionale* is *trah-di-tzee-on-ah'-lay*. Try saying *questa*, *davanti*, and *poliziotti*.

The Italian alphabet has no *k, j, w, x,* or *y,* and *h* is always silent.

Here are a few hints to get you started so you can read this book aloud or to yourself. The former is much more fun.

The vowel sounds are pretty straightforward:

A usually sounds like the *a* in *about*. *Pasta* is *pah'-stah*.

E can sound like the short *e* in *belt*. *Pienza* is *pee-en'-zah*.

E can also sound like the long *a* in *pray*. *Dove* is *doe'-vay*.

(Note that you should always pronounce the *e* at the end of a word).

I sounds like the double *e* in *peek*. *Piccola* is *pee'-koh-lah*.

O sounds like the long *o* in *no*. *Anno* is *ah'-no*.

U sounds like the double *o* in *loop*. *Tutti* is *too'-tee*.

Here are some tips on consonants:

The pronunciation of *c* and *g* depends on the letter that follows it.

If *c* is followed by *a, o, u,* or *h*, it sounds like the *k* in *kangaroo*.

Casa is *kah'-zah*, and *chiudo* is *kee-oo'-doh*.

If *c* is followed by *e* or *i*, it sounds like the *ch* in *church*. *Cittadina* is *chee-tah-dee'-nah*, and *c'è* is *chay*.

If *g* is followed by *a,o,u,*or *h*, it sounds like the *g* in *got*. *Vengono* is *ven'-go-no* and *Margherita* is *mar-geh-ree'-tah*.

If *g* is followed by *e* or *i*, it sounds like the *g* in *gentle*. *Oggi* is *oh'-jee* and *generazioni* is *jen-ay-rah-tzee-o'-nee*.

Finally, a note on a few other letter combinations:

Gli is like the sound in *million*. *Taglio* is *tah'-lyee-oh*.

Gn is like the sound in *onion*. *Sognando* is *sone-yahn'-doh*.

Zz is like the sound in *pizza*. *Pizza* is *piz'-za* is *PIZZA*.

To really learn how to pronounce words in Italian, try watching Italian movies, listening to Italian songs and native speakers, or take a trip to Pienza. *Buon viaggio!*

A Brief History of Pizza

Pizza's exact origins are hard to pinpoint, though most food historians agree that modern pizza was created in Naples, Italy, where it is still a famous local specialty.

Cato the Elder, who wrote the first history of Rome in the second century B.C., described a "flat round of dough dressed with olive oil, herbs, and honey baked on stone." A little later, Virgil (70–19 B.C.) wrote in *The Aeneid* about cakes of bread, "a scenty meal," used as plates and then eaten. Our knowledge of ancient Roman cooking comes mostly from a book written in the first century A.D. by the gourmet Marcus Gavius Apicius that contains recipes for flatbreads with various toppings. And we know something about the tools for making pizza from those excavated at Pompeii, near Naples, buried in the eruption of Mt. Vesuvius in A.D. 79. Around 1830, Alexandre Dumas, a French writer who loved food, wrote about pizza in Naples. He noted that it was the only food of the humble people there in winter. "In Naples, pizza is flavored with oil, lard, tallow, cheese, tomato, or anchovies."

By the eighteenth century, numerous open-air stands and roving vendors in Naples produced and sold slices of pizza cut to the size the customer could afford. Made from a few basic ingredients, it was considered a peasant food, eaten in the street for breakfast, lunch, and dinner by those who had little or no cooking equipment at home. Macaroni – also sold in the street – was a more costly meal, usually reserved for the weekend. In 1830, the Antica Pizzeria Port'Alba, which had been serving pizza in the street for almost one hundred years, opened the first pizzeria in Naples where people could sit down at tables to eat. It is still in business in the original location.

The standard for modern pizza was set in 1889 when Queen Margherita and King Umberto I (ruler of the newly unified Italy), discovered the local dish at a pizzeria called Pietro e Basta Cosi! There, the renowned *pizzaiolo* (pizza-maker), Rafaele Esposito, offered three pizzas to the queen. She had become bored with French cuisine (the standard fare for most of Europe's royalty) and was very interested in local Italian cooking. Her favorite pizza was the one bearing the colors of the new flag of Italy – red (tomato), green (basil), and white (mozzarella cheese), and it was promptly named Pizza Margherita. That pizzeria is still in existence, now called Pizzeria Brandi. Even with royal endorsement though, pizza would not become popular outside of Naples – in Italy or the United States – until after the Second World War.

In the late nineteenth century, about four million Italians came to the United States looking for work. Most of them were from southern Italy. Many found factory jobs in the northeast, where they began making pizza in their new neighborhoods, at home or in rented space in bakeries, mostly for their families. By the early 1900s, they began opening their own bakeries and groceries selling pizza to the wider Italian community. The first "sit-down" pizzeria in the U.S. opened in New York in 1905. Gennaro Lombardi, the proprietor, was a young immigrant from Naples. He mentored many other young men from his hometown who later established some of the finest pizzerias in New York and beyond.

Although there were successful family-owned pizzerias in factory towns all over the northeast United States by the 1920s, pizza didn't really become popular beyond Italian neighborhoods until the mid 1940s. Soldiers returning from the war in Europe had fallen in love with the dish in Italy and couldn't do without it once they came home. From about 1945 until 1960, independent pizzerias opened all over the U.S. They made (or locally sourced) their own ingredients, from dough to sauce to mozzarella and other toppings. Massive brick-lined ovens fueled by coal or wood had to be fired up and tended day and night, even though the pies cooked for only a minute or two. The pizzaioli were venerated for their considerable talents. Making pizza was hard work.

Beginning in the 1960s, the proliferation of pizza chains altered the business irrevocably. In addition to greater demand, the invention of the commercial electric mixer and gas oven encouraged the increasingly widespread pizza business. Pizza became a mass-produced commodity, forcing many independent producers to close up shop. To make matters worse, large numbers of Italian immigrants had begun moving to the suburbs by the 1940s, abandoning the small family-style urban pizzerias. In the twenty-first century, however, a renewed interest in authentic cuisine and local ingredients has produced a renaissance of independent pizzerias offering handmade, high-quality pies, traditional and otherwise.

Neapolitan pizza is still generally considered the world's best pizza, partly because of the high quality of local ingredients and the fact that it is still cooked in extremely hot coal or wood ovens. Its rival, New York-style pizza, is larger but thinner than its Italian cousin. According to the Associazione Verace Pizza Napoletana, established in Naples in 1984, there are only two authentic pies – the Margherita (tomato, mozzarella, olive oil, basil) and the Marinara (tomato, olive oil, oregano, and garlic). Worried that the original pizza pedigree would disappear in a world where pizza is sold on every street corner, the VPN established strict rules governing the ingredients and preparation of true Neapolitan-style pizza. Pizzerias around the world may apply for VPN status if they agree to follow the very detailed guidelines, which cover every aspect of production, from ingredients to shaping and dimensions of the dough, to final baking. In 1997, Neapolitan pizza was granted DOC status (Denominazione di Origine Controllata). This honorary title, given to certain distinguished European foods, guarantees the origin and quality of products like wine and cheese. (The French equivalent is Appellation Contrôlée.) Mozzarella di Bufala Campana has DOC trademark as well. Some pizza aficionados question whether following these (or other government-issued rulings) guarantees a superior product. There are countless variations in the methods and ingredients of pizza wherever it is made.

Here on the facing page is the author's own recipe, yet one more permutation in pizza's long and delicious history.

A Recipe for Pizza Margherita

This recipe can easily be made at home without a lot of equipment. Over the years, I have found that several factors are especially important. First, the dough should be soft, pliable, and as moist as possible – just short of sticky. Second, be sure the water is barely warm – not too hot. Third, if you have the time, let the dough rise for at least an hour (even more) after kneading, and then a second time – after you shape it in the pan – for another hour, before adding any toppings. If necessary, you can cut back on rising time. Also, you'll see that less water is needed on a very humid day, while more water should be used when the air is very dry. Experiment, see what works best for you, and have fun with it!

INGREDIENTS FOR THE DOUGH
(to make two 12-inch pizzas or one large one):

3 cups flour (regular, unbleached)

2¼ teaspoons yeast

1 teaspoon salt

½ teaspoon sugar

approximately 1¼ cup barely warm water with 1 teaspoon olive oil added

INGREDIENTS FOR THE TOPPING:

8 ounces canned San Marzano tomatoes, whole or diced. Drain and crush the tomatoes by hand. You can use fresh ones, but they can be watery.

8 ounces mozzarella. Use either fresh cow's milk mozzarella or *mozzarella di bufala*. Cut into slices or chunks.

a handful of fresh basil leaves

1 tablespoon olive oil

salt to season

Note: In Naples, the pizzas have a sparse amount of tomato and mozzarella. You can, of course, use an infinite variety of other toppings instead of this classic Neapolitan Margherita.

If you are kneading by hand, put all dry ingredients in a large bowl, add the liquid gradually, stirring as best you can with a large spoon until it begins sticking together into a ball. Then dump it out onto a floured surface and knead, constantly folding the dough over onto itself, until smooth and soft. This may take about 10 minutes.

If you are using a food processor, put all dry ingredients in the bowl. With the motor running, add about a cup of the water/oil mixture in a slow, steady stream, then stop the machine and check the dough. If it still feels dry, turn it back on and add more liquid. Keep doing this until it feels soft and forms a ball. Process for about 30 seconds, total. Cover your hands with flour before removing the dough from the processor in case the dough is too sticky to handle.

Put the dough in a greased bowl, turn the dough to oil it all over, then cover the top of the bowl loosely with a plastic bag or plastic wrap. Place a towel over the plastic. If the room is cool, place the bowl with dough over a smaller bowl of warm water. Let the dough rise about an hour, then divide it in two, and let each ball rise again, in separate oiled bowls.

Preheat the oven to 475 degrees. Form each ball of dough into a large, flat disk, place it on a metal sheet with a rim, and spread it out until thin but not too thin. This will take some time, since the dough wants to keep shrinking. Brush the edges with olive oil. Add the toppings and bake for 10 minutes or until the edges and the cheese are nicely browned. Let cool a few minutes before cutting.

Once again, my heartfelt thanks to the most impressive team
at David R. Godine – to David himself, and to Susan Barba, above all.

On the home front, I dedicate the book to
Tom, Eva, and Abel, with love.

Published in 2013 by
David R. Godine, Publisher
Post Office Box 450
Jaffrey, New Hampshire 03452
www.godine.com

Special thanks to Collina Italiana for their assistance
with editing the Italian language text of this book.

LIBRARY OF CONGRESS CATALOGING-IN-PUBLICATION DATA

Fillion, Susan.
Pizza in Pienza / written and illustrated by Susan Fillion.
p.   cm.
Summary: A child who lives in a small town in Italy describes
a favorite food and learns about its history.
ISBN 978-1-56792-459-6 (alk. paper)
[1. Pizza—Fiction. 2. Pienza (Italy)—Fiction. 3. Italy—Fiction.] I. Title.
PZ7.F4953Pi 2012
[E]—dc23
2012005140

FIRST PRINTING
Printed in China

PIZZA IN PIENZA *has been set in Monotype Columbus, a family of types designed by Patricia Saunders to commemorate the five-hundredth anniversary of their namesake's epic journey in search of a westward route to the Indies. The letterforms of these cosmopolitan types derive from two great Spanish printed books of the late fifteenth and early sixteenth centuries: one a collection of the works of Virgil printed by Jorge Coci, the other a calligraphic manual by Juan de Yciar, which featured types by the renowned French punchcutter Robert Granjon and was printed by Coci's son-in-law.* ❧ *In their current form, the Columbus types retain the lively, rather rustic flavor of their models, although the designer has judiciously modified elements that might interfere with comfortable reading. The types' rich color and sturdy forms are adaptable to a variety of books, but seem most at home when a decidedly decorative feel and dense texture are desired.*

DESIGN & COMPOSITION BY
CARL W. SCARBROUGH

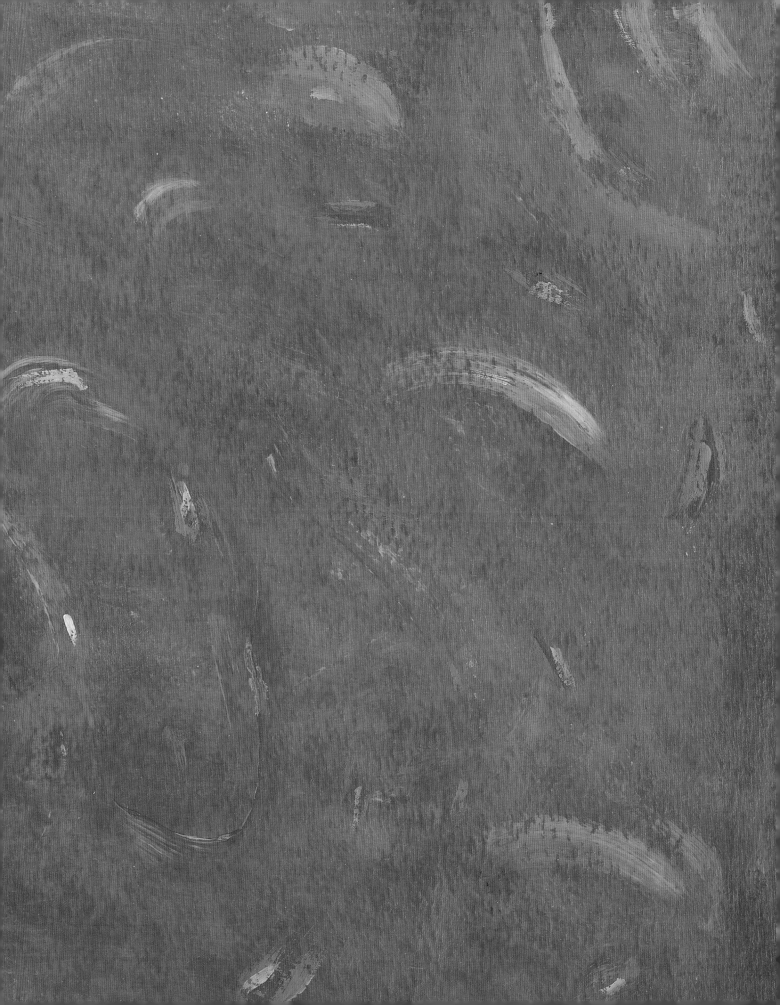